*Tammy T. Cross*

*Anointed Inspirations Publishing*

*Presents*

# How Much Can A Soul

# Take

D1523469

# By: Tammy T. Cross

*How Much Can a Soul Take*

*Tammy T. Cross*

**Copyright © 2018 Tammy T. Cross**
Published by Anointed Inspirations Publishing, LLC

**Note:** This is a work of fiction. Names, characters, places and incidents either are products of the author's imagination or are used fictitiously. Any resemblance to actual events or locales or persons, living or dead, is entirely coincidental

**Anointed Inspirations Publishing, LLC is currently accepting Urban Christian Fiction, Inspirational Romance, Inspirational Poetry, Self-Help, Memoirs, and Young Adult fiction submissions. For consideration please send manuscripts to**

# *Shay*

I had had a long day at work today so coming home plopping down on the couch and kicking off my heels off sure felt good. I am a receptionist at Jones Law Firm here in Bryan, Texas. We get lots of clients coming in on a daily basis and we stay busy. So walking through my living room door sure feels good right about now. As I sat down on my sage sofa I began to reminisce about the things Mitchell and I have been going through this past year. I had two miscarriages and then I found out Mitchell has been cheating on me. I got up and walked into the kitchen and grabbed me a glass from the cabinet and opened the freezer and filled it halfway with ice. I then strolled over to the bar that was sitting next to my kitchen and poured me a glass of Peach Paul Mason.

"Ahhh, that's was just what I needed," I told myself as I pulled the glass away from my lips.

Tammy T. Cross

Drinking seemed to be the only thing to keep my mind off of the pain I have been enduring lately. He says he hasn't been cheating but I can't tell by the way he been strolling in here all times of the night smelling like a fresh bar of Coast soap. I guess since I hadn't been saying anything about it, so it really didn't bother him either when I looked at him crazy as he walked in grabbing his pajamas out of the drawer, sliding them on before jumping into bed.

I tell you this is beginning to be a bit much for me and I swear I am about to let him know how I truly feel about things. I am just waiting for that right moment. I don't know when that moment will be but the way things are going now oh it was bound to come sooner than later. Mitch problem is he knows I will do anything for him. So he uses that to his advantage.

I gave up family and friends for this man and it makes me angry how he treats me. I cook for him make sure his clothes are cleaned and hung up just the way he likes them. When he came home on time I made sure after he has eaten his dinner he had a nice hot bath ran for him. My friends use to say I am too good of a woman but where I am from I use to watch my grandmother do it for my granddaddy clean up until he passed away. My mother still does it for my dad until this day. I am a woman that loves to show my man that he is loved.

# How Much Can a Soul Take

## Tammy T. Cross

We don't even feel like a couple anymore. When he does come in he just climbs on the bed and turns his back and falls fast asleep. I really think he blames me for not being able to carry the babies until full term. Even though he says he doesn't, his actions show me different.

Mitchell is a very handsome guy standing a good six foot one. In fact every time we would go out every woman we passed made sure to turn around and steal a peek at him. He kept his hair cut low and the waves he had in his head most men would die for. His beard was cut low and lined very neatly. It fit right in with his smooth cocoa complexion. I tell you his pearly white teeth are what drew me to him when he smiled at me the day we met.

Don't get me wrong I have good self-esteem and love everything about me. I don't think I have a problem with the way I look at all. I stand every bit of five foot three 135 pounds with hips for days. My hair is naturally curly and so long that it reaches the center of my back. My skin is high yellow; in fact, back in the days, they use to call me Yella Bone. My eyes are hazel and I always got tons of compliments on how beautiful they are.

The biggest problem I have with Mitchell Bradley is that he's a handsome guy and he knows it. He likes to parade around letting me know he wanted to be seen. So when the cheating started it shouldn't have been a surprise to me. I was in denial because I never thought he would ever betray me like that. When we first got together three years ago we were so in love. We would go out to the movies, dinner and even church, which we both really enjoyed most of all.

Sitting here sipping on this drink I almost forgot I had to check on my turkey wings I had cooking in the crockpot. I ran over to the counter next to the sink in the kitchen and pulled the top off of the pot. "Uhmmm that smells so good" I yelled out.

I took a fork and stuck it down in the turkey wing and they were so tender the meat started to fall apart. I dug down deeper in the pot to take a sample of the rice I added to the pot earlier that morning. I wanted to see if I needed to add more seasoning to it but when I tasted it, it just melted in my mouth. The cream of mushroom I added to the pot had my meal tasting so on point.

He promised me that he would come home on time tonight so I wanted to make sure that everything was ready when he came in. I opened up a can of green beans and put them in the pot on the stove. Then I got a slice of bacon out of the refrigerator and browned it in a pan with a small piece of onion. When I got that done I added it to the pot of green beans to give it a little flavor and let them simmer for a bit. Once I was done with that I placed my dinner rolls in a roll basket to put on the dining room table.

## How Much Can a Soul Take

*Tammy T. Cross*

While the beans were simmering I whipped up a pitcher of tropical punch Kool-Aid which was my husband's favorite drink. Then I placed it in the top of the fridge so that it would be cool by the time my husband makes it home. Once I had that all out of the way I walked over to my dining room table and lit the warm brown sugar scented candle and then set the table up so that when he walks in the door everything would be ready.

When all of the food was ready I sat back down on the couch and sipped and waited on Mitch. I looked at my clock and noticed he was now an hour late. I got up and went back to the kitchen and re-warmed the food because I didn't want it to be cold when he walked in. Then I grabbed the bottle and poured me another drink.

After about three hours of waiting, I became frustrated and went ahead and ate without him. I then walked into the kitchen and put away the food. Once I was done I grabbed the candle off the table and walked into the bathroom and place it on the side of the tub. The thoughts that were going through my head were causing me so much pain inside. I grabbed the glass and took a big swig and then sat it back down. I then slid down into the hot bubble bath and rested my head on the back of the tub and relaxed until the water became too cool for me to enjoy anymore. So I rinsed off really well and got out and dressed for bed.

*How Much Can a Soul Take*

*Tammy T. Cross*

I laid in my canopy king size bed alone tossing and turning for hours. I couldn't sleep for the hurt that Mitchell was causing deep inside of me. All at once I heard the key unlocking the door and he came walking in. I was so angry at him I couldn't keep my mouth shut any longer.

"Mitchell, where have you been? I have been waiting for you for hours. You promised that you would be home on time to have dinner with me. I yelled out to him.

"Come on Shay I have had a long day I don't have time for this right now. It is late and all I want to do his go to bed." He shouted back at me.

"Oh no buddy we are going to discuss this right now. I am tired of you putting me through this day after day. Something has got to change Mitch. I feel like you are taking advantage of my kindness."

"Look, like I said before I am tired and I am going to bed this conversation is over," he snapped in a way I have never heard before.

Usually, I wouldn't even bring up a conversation about him coming in late but I wanted answers and I want them now. So I let it all out I didn't care how tired he was. "You tired huh, so you not gonna even shower. Oh, that's right you did that before you got here. I can smell the coast soap all on you."

*Tammy T. Cross*

Before I knew it he jumped up, grabbed me out of bed and lifted me up in the air by my neck. I could see the rage all in his eyes. Whoever this chick was she got him wrapped around her finger because the old Mitchell would never touch me in such a way that he did tonight.

"Mitchell put me down I can't breathe" I manage to yell out.

All at once he let go and I fell flat out on the floor gasping for air. I laid there and cried asking God what did I do for him to treat me in such a way. After pulling myself together I looked up and he was grabbing his keys and walking back out the door, without saying one word to me.

I ran in behind him begging him not to leave. When I made it to the door he was slamming it in my face. I placed my back up against the door and slid all the way down to the floor crying my eyes out.

*"Look, God, I don't know what I did to be treated this way. I have bent over backward for this guy just for him to step all over me like trash. Lord, I need your help. I am trying to be a faithful wife and play my part in this marriage. Why can't my husband play his part?"* I laid on the floor and vented to God

I got up off of the floor and made my way to the bathroom to wash my face. When I was done I crawled into bed and buried myself deep under the covers until I was fast asleep. The next morning I felt so bad there was no way I could go to work.

"Hello, Karla this is Shay can you let my supervisor Jack know that I won't make it into work today, I am not feeling well."

"Oh no you never call in. You must be really sick, I hope you feel better soon and yes ma'am I will tell him, Karla replied right before hanging up.

I hung the phone up and lay back down. I didn't want to be bothered at all. After all that drinking last night my head is pounding like crazy. I think that is what gave me the courage to go in so hard on Mitchell. Truth be told Paul is not the reason I have to take responsibility for that, this was a situation well overdue. I needed that to all come out. Even if it did cause me to almost be choked to death.

I laid around half the day and I felt like it was time for me to pull myself together and get out of this bed. I rolled out of the bed like a zombie and made my way to the bathroom to clean myself up. Once I was done I went into the living room and turned the televisions on. I flipped from channel to channel before I settled on just watching *"The Bold and The Beautiful."*

I got into the show so deep I almost didn't hear my phone ringing. It was Brent an old friend of mine from back in the day. About five years ago he moved away with my God sister Jenny.

*How Much Can a Soul Take*

*Tammy T. Cross*

They got married and had a beautiful baby boy name Jaylon. Every time he is in town we meet up and have lunch and catch up on lost time which wasn't too often.

"Brent, how are ya? It is so nice to hear your voice." I said with excitement in my voice as I answered the phone.

"Hi, I'm good. 'I'm in town I was wondering if we could meet for lunch today. I got to fill you in on how things have been going with me. I also need to see how you have been doing." Brent replied.

"Sure, I can meet you at Cheddars in about ten minutes if that's fine with you."

"That will be perfect, see you then," said Brent.

I turned the television off and went to my bathroom to look myself over. My face looked so puffy from crying so I applied a little makeup to make it not so noticeable. I looked at my neck and saw that it was a little bruised from Mitchell choking me. I applied a little foundation to my neck to hide that as well. I didn't want to upset Brent. He has always been so protective of me ever since we were younger.

He and I lived down the street from one another as kids and our moms were just like sisters so you can imagine just how close we were. We were just like cousins and he never let anyone in the neighborhood pick on me.

*Tammy T. Cross*

After I got myself together I grabbed my keys and headed out to go and meet Brent. I was so excited to see him that I couldn't wait until I got to the restaurant. I had so much I needed to talk to him about. Today started out rough but now that my old friend was in town it couldn't have been better.

# *Mitchell*

Who does Shay think she is questioning me about where I been. Yeah, I did tell her I was going to come home on time tonight but after hearing this night after night you would think she knew better than to believe that by now. I am so over her right now she wants me to believe she had a miscarriage with my babies but I knew that wasn't true. I knew she wasn't ready for children but I was ready to settle down and raise a nice little family with her trifling behind.

Shay thinks that if she had a baby it would mess up her little figure but I wasn't with her for her figure. I was in love with her. I thought she was a beautiful person on the inside not just on the outside but she fooled me. Yes, I still love my wife but I am not in love with her like I was when we first got married. Thanks to her for messing that all up.

She is always trying to run to God like he going to help her but he is not going to help someone that can't be truthful. I was always taught the bible says "Thy Shall Not Lie" and she such a liar in my eyes. True the bible also says not to judge anyone but I am just saying what I know about my wife. I hate to talk about her in such a way but she upsets me to the core.

I had no right to choke her but the old folks use to say the truth hurts and I guess when she called me out on smelling like Coast bath soap that hit a nerve. See I met this girl that comes into town from time to time and we started out as friends but after some time things got kinda serious between us.

I was out eating lunch one day at *On the Border* when this beautiful lady come strutting in the door. She had her long beautiful hair down and a gray business suit on that fit her body very well. The way she walked in those heels would make you think she was walking the catwalk for a modeling agency. Her skin was as smooth as a milk chocolate bar. The little bit of makeup she had on really highlighted her face just right. Not that she needed makeup because she was pretty without it and her Chinese looking eyes were to die for.

When she walked in I overheard her tell the waiter that she was dining alone. They were walking past my table when I stopped them and said, "I overheard you telling the waiter you were dining alone and I don't mind if you join me I am also dining alone"

She looked down at me with a beautiful smile and responded, "I don't mind if I do."

After introducing herself to me and telling me her name was Shonda Davidson, we ordered our food and talked for a good thirty minutes before I had to get up and return to work. I called the waiter over and paid for our food and exchanged numbers with her. I told her we needed to keep in touch because I really enjoyed her company. She agreed and we headed our separate ways and hadn't talked since that day.

I was sitting at my desk about a month later when the phone went off. "Hey beautiful how are you," I said upon answering the phone.

"Hey there handsome, I am just fine just wanted you to know that I am in town for a few hours and I was hoping that I could see you," she responded.

"Sure that would be great, I am wrapping up here at work and I can meet you in a bit. Where are you located?" I asked her

"I am at the Best Western motel off of University Drive. I am in room 312, Shonda responded.

"Cool, give me fifteen minutes and I am there.

I clicked the button to log out of my computer and grabbed my keys from inside my desk and headed over to the motel where she was. When I got there she opened the door wearing a nice blue baby doll dress. The way she looked in it would make any man sin. I tried to look her in her face instead of looking at her lovely body but that was very hard for me to do.

"Are you going to just stand there and look at me or are you going to come over here and have a seat." She asked me now sitting on the little sofa patting the empty spot next to her.

"Oh umm, yes I said walking fast over to the couch to have a seat next to her. I told her now as nervous as ever.

"So Mitchell, how has your day been?" She asked now smiling like an angel from the heavens above.

I was so mesmerized by her smile that I found it hard to speak. She had two golds on her canine teeth with diamonds all around them that sparkled every time she smiled.

"Mitchell, calm down I am not going to bite, you don't have to be so nervous," she giggled and said.

"I am sorry I just can't get over how beautiful you are. Every time I try to get a word out I look into your eyes and you just take my breath away."

"You are very handsome yourself," she licked her lips and slid in close to me and said.

The moment she said that I just wanted to reach out to grab her and take her to paradise. Before I knew it she had her lips on mine and there was no way I could pull mine away. After rolling around for about an hour we were both laying there in disbelief. I looked up and knew God was disappointed with me but this woman had me out of my mind and I was enjoying every minute of it.

I rolled over onto my back and we talked for another hour until she said she had to be getting back home. She said she was in town for a photo shoot for Essence Magazine. I didn't really know what kind of work she did so I took her word for it. Looking at this woman I just knew she was a model, so to find out she was modeling for different magazines wasn't a surprise to me. After we got up and washed each other off she headed home and so did I.

When I looked at the time I knew that Shay would be upset but I didn't care about her anymore. I don't know why she won't just pack up and leave. I can't have my Pastor thinking I was the bad person for leaving my wife. If she goes I could tell him I tried but she gave up on me. Then ask God to forgive me later.

A few months have passed and Shonda and I had been really enjoying each other's company. After all of the late night coming in Shay still had hope for our marriage. Until one night I came in late after she had cooked a nice meal for us and she tried to check me about breaking my promise. She even had the nerve to question me about what I smell like. I mean I do feel bad about grabbing her by her neck but now she knows how I feel, just like I did when she got rid of my babies.

Shonda said she couldn't make it back to town for the next few months so I started going home on time at night. After all that I did to Shay, she still fixed my dinner like a good wife would do. I tell you the way she treated me I was starting to become torn between my feelings for her and Shonda. My wife is as sexy as Shonda and the way she been parading around the house in her little tee shirt nightgown, has me feeling some type of way.

I finally pulled her to the side to apologize for the way I had been treating her. "Look, Shay, I know that I have been treating you badly lately but I been under a lot of stress." I lied and told her.

"All you had to do was talk to me about it Mitch. I would have understood. Taking your problems out on me is never a way to solve a problem babe," she responded.

"Yeah I know but I was so stressed I couldn't control myself, babe," I told her now pulling her close kissing her on her neck.

I must have hit her spot because for the next couple of hours we were feeling like we were at the pearly gates of heaven. By the way, she was crying I know she really needed me in this way. I had been neglecting her mentally and sexually and that is never a good thing for a man to do to his wife. I know I been out doing my thang but it would hurt me find out my wife is slipping out on me. I may front like I don't care and want her to leave but truth be told the way she making me feel right now I couldn't handle her leaving.

We climbed out of bed and showered together which is something we hadn't done in forever. When we were done we went back into the bedroom and I laid across the bed while she rubbed me down with some warm massaging oil. Man, I felt so relaxed. Next thing I know I was out for the night. When I woke up the next morning she was curled up in my arms asleep looking so beautiful. I didn't want to wake her so I just laid there and let her sleep a little while longer.

Thirty minutes later she was squirming around in the bed so I kissed her on the head and said, "Morning sleepy head, how did you sleep last night?

"Morning babe I have to say I haven't slept that good in a long time," she responded kissing me back.

"Girl, go take care of that morning breathe, you killing me right now," I jokingly told her.

"Mitch, do not play with me and that's what woke me up I smelled yours breathing over me while I was sleeping." She said as she slid out of bed and ran toward the bathroom as I threw a pillow pretending to hit her with it.

After we were all cleaned up I got dressed and headed out the door heading to work. All the way to work I couldn't help but think about the night my wife and I just have. Shonda crossed my mind a few times but I brushed it off real quick. I enjoyed Shay so much I think I am going to break it off with Shonda and focus on mine and my wife's relationship. It won't be easy telling Shonda about Shay after all of this time of messing around but hey I don't know what or who she's with when she's not with me. I was thinking about Shay and Shonda so much I didn't realize I had made it to my office this fast. Even though I was still tired from last night and could use a little more rest I went on in to get my day started.

# *Shay*

I pulled into Cheddars and had a huge smile on my face when I spotted Brent, standing in front of his 2016 candy apple red Chevy Silverado. I found the nearest parking spot that I could find. I jumped out of my black Chrysler 300 and ran and hugged Brent so hard I almost knocked him over.

"Hold up girl your short self is very strong. You almost made me lose my balance girl, He said leaning up against his truck trying to break his fall.

"Sorry, it's just that I haven't seen you in so long and it is so nice to finally get to see you again," I told him

"It's good to see your cute self to Shay. Girl you haven't changed one bit, them hips looks like they have gotten a little wider but don't get me wrong it looks good on you." He said looking and checking me out.

"Stop it boy, come on let's go in here and grab a bit to eat I am hungry as a horse."

I grabbed him by the hand and led him in. The waitress seated us in a corner at a little booth big enough for the both of us.

"Hi, my name is Talia I will be your waitress today. What would you two like to drink?" She asked us while handing us a menu to look over.

"I would like a strawberry mango swirl," I told her.

"I will have what she is having ma'am," Brent said.

"I will be back with your beverages in a moment. I will take your order when I return," Talia said to Brent and me.

We nodded our heads and she left the table.

"So what are you going to be getting today?" Brent asked me.

"I think I will be getting potato soup with a house salad. How about you," I asked him?

"Well I think I will get my usual chicken fried steak, mashed potatoes, and the sweet carrots," he responded.

"That sounds good but if I eat that heavy I won't have room for dinner tonight. I have to make sure Mitchell has a nice meal when he gets off work tonight and I can't have him eating alone." I told Brent.

After I said that I noticed Brent had gotten really quiet. After sitting there for a minute with no one saying anything the waitress walked up with our drinks and asked," are you to ready to order or do you guys need a minute more."

"No we are ready, Brent spits out. I will have a chicken fried steak, mashed potatoes, and the sweet carrots. She will have the potato soup and house salad," Brent told the waiter and handed her both of our menus.

"Brent, why do you always do that?" I asked him.

"Do what?" He asked as if he didn't already know what I was going to say.

"Order for me. I can speak for myself," I fussed at him.

"It's a habit I am sorry. I didn't mean anything by it," He told me.

Once again the silence found our table. We both sat and sipped on our drinks before I started getting this weird vibe coming from him and I couldn't take it no more before I asked him, "What's wrong, why did you get quiet after I said Mitchell's name."

"Shay, it's just I can't believe after all he has put you trough you're still with him," He said to me.

"Oh now don't start we go through this every time we meet up. You got to understand that is my husband and I am being faithful and doing my part in this marriage. God wouldn't like it if

I treated him like he does me. I have to let God fight that battle for me." I told him.

"That may be true but I know God will forgive you if you leave him. God doesn't want you to be no fool either." He said sending me in defense mode.

"Brent Davidson I can't believe you said that to me. So you think I am a fool?" I asked him now so angry with tears were rolling down my cheeks.

"Come on girl I would never call you that. You know me better than that. I was simply saying he wouldn't want you to be one and stay in a relationship that some guy keeps dogging you out." He said while sliding his chair around close to me wiping the tears from my face with his thumb.

I quickly pulled myself together to receive my food that the waitress was now bringing to our table. "Is there anything else you two need? The waitress asked. I quickly nodded no and she walked away.

I had a lot on my mind so I just ate without saying a word and Brent ate his food and watched me like he was trying to read my mind. He could tell I was still in my feeling so he stopped eating and grabbed my hands and said, " I am sorry I never meant to hurt you. I just hate to see someone run over you. I have known you since we were kids and I really care for you."

*Tammy T. Cross*

Sitting here looking and listening to every word he was saying gave me a feeling that he was talking about something more deeper than caring for me as a friend. I just brushed it off because we grew up like cousins and I knew he couldn't possibly be looking at me in that way. This drink is a little strong so I could be reading him wrong because I was starting to feel a little tipsy.

We finished up our food he invited me to go hang out with me in his room and talk more because we couldn't talk like he wanted with a restaurant full of people. He paid for our ticket, left a tip and I followed him back to his room. When we made it there I was really feeling that mixed drink. He grabbed my hand and led me in. When we got in the room I kicked my shoes off and made myself at home because my feet were hurting so badly.

"Well I see I don't have to tell you to make yourself comfortable," Brent chuckled.

"Boy I couldn't take those shoes any longer," I told him taking the glass of *Moscato* he poured for me.

We have been sitting here talking about old times for a few hours now but I could tell that it was something bothering him and he wasn't telling me everything. So I knew it was left up to me to get it out of him.

"Okay, spit it out. I know you are hiding something from me and it's time you let it out." I told him as I sit up on the bed with my legs now crossed in Indian style waiting for him to start talking.

He sits up and put his head down and gripping the top of his head with the palm of his hand. "I think my wife has been stepping out on me. I can't prove it but I have this gut feeling. I was always told to go with my gut and if she is Shay I don't know what I will do." Brent said with an evil look in his eye.

"My God sister loves you. She would never mess around with anyone else." I said praying that I was right because she always was a little friendly back in the days.

I guess he must've gotten hot because he pulled his navy blue polo shirt off and threw it on the bed. Boy, I tell you he had a six pack for days. His body was so fit and this six foot two dark chocolate man was looking mighty nice to me right now. He had muscles so big you could tell he worked out often. I just bit my top lip and put my head down. I am a married woman and I shouldn't be looking at this man in such a way but I couldn't help but catch a peek every chance I got.

"Oh yeah, do you want to explain all the so-called business trips she has been taking lately and packing around her cell phone every move she takes while we are at home. If she goes to the bathroom her phones go with her. Shay, she never did that before." he blurted out to me.

*How Much Can a Soul Take*

*Tammy T. Cross*

I sit back and thought about Mitchell and how when he first started cheating how he started doing the same thing. He would always keep his phone on vibrate and keep it turned face down. Even though I felt uneasy about it I just pushed it to the back of my brain.

"I'll call and talk to her and find out what's going on. I know there has to be a good explanation for this. Maybe its business and you are taking it the wrong way. I mean she does work for the FBI. I said trying to get him to agree with me.

"You could be right about that but I still feel like it's something more to it. She doesn't get moved by me anymore and she has been acting kind of strange when I question her about it. I get lucky if she gives in and gives me a little bit of her, you know what I mean. I think I am losing my wife," he said now fighting back the tears.

I leaned in and hugged him trying to comfort him but I guess we both had, had one too many glasses of wine because one thing led to another and an hour later we were both waking up with nothing on. I looked at Brent and knew we had done wrong. I threw my clothes on, grabbed my purse and keys not saying a word to him. I ran out the door and jumped in my car and drove straight home.

When I made it home I ran into the house dropped my purse and keys on the bed and went straight to the shower. I knew I had betrayed my God sister by sleeping with her husband. *"Lord please forgive me. I never meant for this to happen. Lord if you forgive me I promise I will never do anything like this again."* I had to pray to God because I knew I overstepped my boundaries and this could never happen again.

When I stepped out of the shower and finished putting on my clothes I picked up my cell phone and saw that I have missed several calls from Brent. Since I didn't answer he decided to text me saying, "Shay I am sorry this happened. I never meant for it to go this far. All I wanted was to talk to you about my marriage and now I may have messed up a childhood friendship with my best friend."

I can't ignore him forever I have to talk to him and let him know that we are just like family and we can never speak of this ever again. I picked up the phone and called him. "Brent we need to talk," I said to him.

"Yes we do," he replied.

"If we want to continue to hang out, we have to just hang out as friends only and that means no sleeping together ever. You are married and so am I. If this gets back to either one of them our marriages will be over." I told him.

"Even though I believe my marriage is already over I agree. I wouldn't want to ruin yours because mine is done with. I respect you too much to hurt you and your husband. I am going back to Chicago tomorrow so I am going to tell you goodbye now," he told me.

I agreed with him and said goodbye as I ended the call. I sat there silent with the phone planted up against my chest when Mitchell walked in the door. I turned and looked around at him with my mouth open as if I had just seen a ghost.

# *Brent*

All the way home my mind was racing thinking about what just transpired between Shay and I. I know it was wrong but she had to know this was bound to happen sooner or later. I have been had it out for her since we were kids but because we grew up so close she never showed that type of interest in me. I came close to telling her years ago but that's when she told me that she was engaged to be married to Mitchell Bradley.

You see I have known that cat for a while. He was my cousin Thomas's best friend. He was always a ladies' man back in the days. He and my cousin use to always make bets on who could get a score with certain girls and of course, Mitchell would always win because he was better looking than Thomas.

When I found out he made a bet on whether he could get with Shay or not I was furious with Thomas. He knew how I felt about her and by the time I tried to warn her it was too late because they had already had one date when I found out. I knew if I would have tried to say anything at this point she would just accuse me of being jealous.

I know that I am not right in a way because the only reason I ended up hooking up with Jenny, Shay's God sister was because she and Shay were so much alike in so many ways. I couldn't have Shay so I settled for Jenny but after some time I grew to love her for her. After a few years of being together, we had a beautiful baby boy name Jaylon. Jaylon is my everything and I wouldn't trade him for the world.

Jenny is a beautiful independent woman that works for the FBI. She has beautiful long hair but wears a weave faithfully. She has a caramel skin tone with lovely hazel Chinese looking eyes. She has long beautiful legs that any man would love to rub on. When she walks she has the strut of Tara Banks. Her skin color was so nice she didn't have to wear much make-up at all. Jenny was every man's dream in my eyes. Even though she wasn't who I wanted at the beginning of our relationship I am glad she is my wife today at least at one time I was.

I was so happy to be home I didn't know what to do. I was tired from the long drive home. When I walked through the door the first person I saw was my son. "Hey little man you missed daddy," I asked him all while giving him the biggest hug.

"Yes, sir I am so glad you are home. I am hungry can you fix me something to eat daddy." My son asked me looking all sad.

"Sure son but where is your mother?" I asked him wondering why my son hasn't eaten.

"She is the room on the phone. Daddy, she has been on the phone all day and I am hungry and you know how she feels about me going in the kitchen trying to fix my own food even though I'm nine years old." He told me and I became upset and had to get to the bottom of this.

I dropped my bags on the floor in the living room and headed straight for the bedroom. When I made it in the room she was lying flat on her stomach with her feet curled up in the air smiling and talking away until she noticed I was in the room.

"I will call you back in a little bit." She told the person on the other end of the receiver.

"So was that call that important that you couldn't feed my son Jenny?" I fussed.

"You can start by lowering your tone Brent and it is not that late." She said looking down at her watch realizing it was 1:30 p.m. in the evening and her child hadn't eaten all day.

"Yeah it's 1:30 in the afternoon and this poor child is so hungry that he's in tears but you go back to your phone call that you were enjoying so much." I turned around and walked out of the room slamming the door behind me.

"Put on your shoe's son you and I are going out to eat, just father and son. How would you like that?" I asked him trying to sound as if everything was okay.

"I would really like that daddy," Jaylon said with the biggest smile on his face.

I grabbed my keys off of the key rack and the two of us walked out the garage got in my BMW instead of my truck and headed over to Chucky Cheese. This was my son's favorite place to go and it would give me some time to think while he plays after we eat.

Jenny had to be feeling guilty because she was blowing up my phone like crazy. At this time she and I have absolutely nothing to talk about. I know that call wasn't business but she thinks she's playing me for a fool right now. Lord if I find out this woman cheating on me it is going to be hell to tell the captain.

Times like this I wish I could pick up the phone and call my friend Shay but I may have ruined that. I sat lost in my thoughts and I didn't notice that Jenny had found us and was now standing directly in my face.

"So why aren't you answering my calls. You should have known I was going to show up here. After all this is one of

Jaylon's favorite places to eat." She said as she stood looking down at me.

"What is it that you could possibly want? The whole time I was gone you never once called me. I'm normally the one to call you but I didn't call just to see if you even cared if I was gone or not." I told her letting out my true feeling.

"Don't give me that, you knew I was busy." Before she could say another word I went in on her.

"Busy, you call laying across the bed with your feet twirled up in the air chatting on the phone with God knows who while my son is starving. Girl, you better get it together before I take my son and leave you by yourself." I told her so loud the whole restaurant including my son had to stop and turn around to look at us.

She had me so heated at the moment I walked over to my son grabbed him by the hand and we stormed out of Chucky Cheese. When we got in the car I speed off so fast I left her standing in the parking lot looking like a fool. People were peeking all out of the windows trying to see what all the fuss was about.

When we got down the road a bit I looked over at Jaylon and he was staring me down with tears filling up in his eyes. It hurt me something terrible to see my son in so much pain. I couldn't even say anything right now because I was still so upset. I did, however, build up enough strength to tell him, "Everything is going to be alright son. "Never once did I take my eyes off the road. I was ashamed for losing my cool in front of all those people in that restaurant.

I pulled up on the red light my head was still spiraling out of control. I heard a horn blow and I looked to the right side of me and Pastor Clark was parked next to me. I rolled the window down and shouted, "Hello Pastor."

"How's your day going?" Looks like you got something heavy on your mind there boy." The Pastor said as if he could read my thoughts.

"Yes Sir, I can't lie I got a lot on my mind right now," I admitted not wanting to lie to the man of God.

"Well I am on my way down to the church follow me we can talk. I have my grandson Tyler in the backseat and he and Jaylon can play while we talk." He told me and pointing in the back seat all at the same time.

The light changed and I looked over my shoulder and saw that it was ok for me to switch lanes and follow him over to New Hope Missionary Baptist Church. We drove about five more miles before we were pulling up at the church. Some of the members were there cleaning the church for Sunday's service. When we got out the car Pastor walked straight up to Mother Brown and ask her to keep an eye on the boys for us and then motioned for me to come to his office.

"Brent take a seat," he said to me as he pointed to an old wooden chair that was sitting in the front of his desk.

I sat down and my heart instantly started to beat really fast because I knew I have to reveal everything to the Pastor. The part I don't know how I am going to explain is me sleeping with Shay. I was starting to feel bad because what I am mad at Jenny about is the same sin I just committed with another woman. I trust him so I will just let it out and let him tell me what I should do.

"So can you tell me what is bothering you," the Pastor asked me.

I put my head down and rubbed the top of my head like I always do when I get stressed.

" I think I am losing my wife and on top of that I go out of town and come back she on the phone with her feet propped up and my son hasn't eaten all day," I shout out all at once.

"Wait a minute son you have to feed this to me one thing at a time. I know your mind is going in circles but if you want me to understand you, you have to tell me in a way I will understand what you are saying."

"This is the problem, Jenny has been all of a sudden for the past month taking a lot of so-called business trips. Now I know her job does call for her to take trips from time to time but this is different. She used to just put her phone down and walk out of the room and leave it but now she packs it around every move she makes." I told Pastor Clark.

"Hmmm, I see where you are going. Let me ask you this Brent. Has she said that she has been working on a big case or has the job been calling on her a lot lately? I am asking because I don't want you to be making something out of nothing." He said trying to understand what the problem really was.

"No, and that's the thing when she had big cases she would talk to me about it without giving out personal details but now we don't even talk anymore. She is always so tired now. I prayed to God for a spirit of discernment a long time ago and I believe God gave me just what I asked for. Pastor, I know something isn't right." I said now looking him straight in the eyes.

"I see why you feel this way Brent and you may be right but you have to keep praying and let God handle this. Remember the old people say what's done in the dark comes to the light."

"You are right and as hard as it may be I know I have to be obedient," I said still scared to tell him about Shay and me.

"Now Brent I know I may not be the smartest man alive but I feel you have more to tell me. You see I prayed for a spirit of discernment and God gave it to me a long time ago. I am listening so let it out." He said as he sits back in his chair and folded his arm like he already knew I had done wrong to.

"I took a deep breath and said, "I don't remember if I told you about my childhood friend Shay. Well, I went to Bryan, Texas to go meet her and tell her about all of my problems. Well we went out to eat went back to my room to talk and one thing led to another and we woke up and an hour later with nothing one." I looked up at him with shame written all over my face after telling him this.

The pastor stood up walked around the desk and shut his office door. He didn't want any of this information to be overheard by anyone that was there cleaning the church. When he sat back down he sits and looked at me for a minute without saying a word. I don't know if he was praying or trying to think of the right words to say to me.

"I looked at him and said, "Pastor say something I know you have something to say."

"Do I really have to say anything, you know what you did was absolutely wrong. I will say this, how can you expect the Lord to do something for you if you are doing wrong."

"Yes, that is the same thing Shay said. When we woke up she ran out and I thought I was never going to see or hear from her ever again. When she called me back she told me we could never hook up in that way anymore if I wanted to remain friends with her. She said that if our spouses found out it could mess up both of our marriages." I told Pastor Clark.

"Brent I am not judging you but you have no right at all to be mad at Jenny. You also cheated even if it did happen one time. The truth of the matter is you did to her exactly what she did to you," The Pastor said and I couldn't argue with that.

"Pastor the worst part about this story is that Shay is Jenny's God sister."

"Good God all mighty Brent you do know that this is going to get messy before it gets better. Lord, I am going to have to pray hard for you young folks. Come on let's pray before I let you go. Oh and stop acting up with Jenny because you think she is cheating. It could be her job that got her acting so strange; besides you are the one that cheated." He said as he walked around the desk and stood right before me.

"Bow your head son let us pray, "*Father God I come to you right now and ask that you step in and take control of this situation. These couples may be going through some milestones right now but I know this is only a test. They have to be the ones that have to prove that they can pass this to move on and have a happy and healthy marriage. Lord for the sins that already been committed by them I ask that you forgive them and help them to move on in life. Lord they can't do it without you. Lord, you are a good God and can move mountains that others think are impossible, so I know that you already got this situation taken care of if they just have faith and believe in you to do so. In Jesus name Amen."*

"*Amen,*" I said when he was done.

"Now go home and work this thing out with your wife. You don't want to throw your marriage down the drain. I don't know what happened you two were so in love. Fix it Brent and bring your marriage back to life like it was years ago.

"Yes Sir, and thanks for the talk I feel so much better.

I gave him a hug and turned and walked out of the office. I went out to the front of the church and saw Jaylon still playing with Tyler and yelled for him to come on so that we can go home. When we got in the car I thought about everything the Pastor Clark said to me while Jaylon talked away about all the things he and Tyler had done.

We finally made it home when we walked through the door Jenny was sitting on the couch looking hurt. I told Jaylon to go to his room and play his game or watch a movie for a while. Hard as it was I knew that I had to be obedient and do as the Pastor had instructed me to do. I walked over to her and apologized for the way I acted. She looked at me and I could see the tears forming up in her eyes. I reached out and grabbed her and pulled her close. I then wiped away the single tear that escaped her eye and the next thing I knew I had kissed her on her plump lips. After that, we found ourselves in our bedroom being fruitful hoping maybe we will get lucky enough to multiply.

# *Mitchell*

"What's wrong babe, why you sitting there looking like you have seen a ghost." I walked in and asked Shay.

"I can't believe you came home tonight on time that's all. I didn't even get to fix you dinner," she said.

"That's okay baby we can go out for dinner tonight. After all, it has been a long time since we had a night out together." I told her as I strolled over and kissed my beautiful wife.

"Well on that note let me grab my purse and I will be ready," Shay said as I watched her hips shift from side to side as she walked to the bedroom to retrieve her purse.

When she returned into the room I led her out to the car and we drove over to Red Lobster for her favorite dish, shrimp scampi. She loved the noodles more than anything. When she first got me to try it I hesitated but one taste and I was in love with that dish. The food was so good I could have licked the plate but I didn't want to embarrass Shay.

When we got there I wanted her to feel loved so I wouldn't let her get out the car until I opened the door for her. I led her right on into the restaurant and even pushed her chair up for her like I did on our first date. I could see the happiness that consumed my wife's eyes. I had neglected her for too long it's time I stop playing around on a good woman and be the man she needs me to be in her life.

I sat at the table and held her hand and gazed into her eyes a moment before the waiter walked over to take our order. "Hello I am Max your waiter, can I start your order off with something to drink." The waiter said standing over us with his pad to write down what we wanted.

"Yes you can get us both a sweet tea and we are also ready to order," I told the waiter waiting to let me know he was ready to take our order. You could tell he was a new employee by the way he was shaking and it took him forever to write down two glasses of tea.

Once he looked up I slowly told him we need two shrimp scampi with pasta and a salad. Even with me saying it slow it still took Max ten minutes to write the order down. I was praying that as nervous as he is that he get our food right because as hungry as I am I would hate to have to get the little fellow fired on his first day of work.

Shay noticed I was getting a little uneasy about our waiter so she grabbed him by the arm before he left and said, "Max calm down you're doing a great job." Is this your first day on the job?"

"Yes ma'am it is" the young man answered.

"You mean to tell me they don't have someone in here training you," she asked the waiter.

"The first part of the day I did but we got so busy the boss said this was a good time to go on the floor by myself and try it on my own," Max replied.

"Well calm down buddy you don't want the customers to see that you are nervous. Slow down, take your time and you will be just fine." I told him as he nodded and walked away to put in our orders.

"I feel kind of bad now, I was just about ready to call management and get that young man fired. That goes to show you can't make a move without getting all the details in a situation."

"I am so glad you didn't, I would hate to see that boy lose his job," she told me.

A few minutes later Max walked back over to the table and brought our drinks. I could tell the talked helped because this time he seems much more comfortable and he was now wearing a smile on his face.

"I will be back with your dinner in a minute," Max told Shay and me.

Not a minute later he was walking out with a huge platter with our food. To my surprise, he had everything we ordered correctly. We thanked him for our food and he walked away as we began to eat.

"Mmmhmm I had forgotten just how delicious this meal was," Shay said stuffing her mouth with her eyes close covering her mouth with one hand to keep anything from falling out of her mouth.

I looked at her a smiled thinking in my head, *"Dang, this high yella hazel eyed girl is so beautiful."* I wanted to talk to her about trying to have another baby but things are going so good I am scared it may cause problems in our relationship again. We have gotten to a good place this last month I would hate to have to ruin what we have going on right now. Well maybe not all the way good but to a place where we are being more open with each other.

"Mitchell what is it, why are you looking at me like that. I know you and the look on your face is telling me you have something that you want to say." Shay said to me breaking me out of my thought.

"It's nothing bae let's just enjoy our meal," I told her trying to smile hoping to wipe away the frown that was forming on her face.

"No, whatever it is just say it. I don't want us to hide anything that needs to be said from each other." She said not knowing what kind of conversation she was pushing me to strike up.

"I know we had problems in the past but I want us to try for another baby. You know how bad I want to start a family bae." I said putting down my fork and grabbing both of her hand, while once again gazing into her eyes.

She dropped her head and I knew this was a conversation that she was dreading to have. Things were going so good between us that I didn't want to ruin a perfect night. I thought to myself if she didn't want to talk about it I wouldn't push the issue. The words she said next just blew my mind into a thousand pieces.

"Mitchell if that's what you really want I am willing to give it one more shot. If this pregnancy doesn't work out I am done. My body can't take anymore bae," Shay replied.

I jumped up in excitement so quick before I knew it I had made it around to Shay's side of the table and picked her up in the air and twirled her around. Everyone in the restaurant had all eyes on us. "Mitch everyone is staring at us can you please put me down," Shay said with the look of embarrassment on her face.

I motioned for the waiter paid my bill and grabbed my wife by the hand and scurried out the door very fast. It didn't take me any time to make it home I was driving so fast. I was glad the police weren't out or I would have had a hefty ticket to pay. When I made it home I rushed around to the passenger side of the car and carried my wife all the way inside the house.

"Uhmm Mitchell, what is this all about?" Shay said as if I had done something that scared her.

*Tammy T. Cross*

"Look I don't want to waste no time. I want to get started on a son or daughter." I told her as she stood there with her mouth wide open.

Not saying another word we headed straight to the room and enjoyed each other's love all night. This woman got me feeling like a million bucks right now and I could tell she is feeling the same by the way she is lying in bed stroking the back of my neck and holding me tight while I rested my head in the middle of her chest trying to catch my breath. Before long the both of us had drifted off into a deep sleep.

When morning came we got up and took a long hot steamy shower together. I washed her back and she washed mine. For the first time in a long time, we felt like husband and wife once again. Once we were done we dried off, got dressed and brushed our teeth, we made breakfast together. She cooked the pan sausage while I made my famous homemade pancakes. We also whipped up some eggs and grits.

When all of that was ready she poured us some orange juice while I fixed our plates. After we were seated, I grabbed my wife's hand and blessed the food. "Man I have forgotten how delicious these pancakes could be," Shay says chewing on a piece of her pancake looking like she had just tasted a piece of heaven.

"Girl you are just hungry they can't be that good. You look like you have tasted a dish from the table at the last supper." I giggled and told her.

"Now see you about to get struck down with your jokes. Remember God sees and hears all." She said moving back like she was looking for a strike of lighting.

"Hey God made me so I know He has to have a sense of humor somewhere deep within Him," I replied.

"I suppose you are right but you need to be wrapping it up honey you got a job you need to be getting to. Unlike me, I have the day off so I can lie around and get some more rest. Lord knows after last night I could use it." Shay said kissing me goodbye as I hurried out the door looking at the time on my watch.

I jumped in my car and went speeding down highway 6. Two minutes away from home my phone began to ring. Thinking it was my wife without looking at the screen I answered it. The voice I heard on the other end made my stomach cringe.

# *Shay*

For the last past few months' things have been going great for me and my husband. He has been coming in on time at night and eating dinner with me like a real family again. I guess my prayers were making it past the ceiling after all. I had gotten to the lowest point in my life and thought that our relationship had gone downhill. I don't know what will happen if I can't give Mitchell a child, but I am going to believe in God and hope for the best.

My husband was the only child and he never had a chance to bond with a brother or a sister. His mother wanted other children but she had health problems that forbid her to have any more children. With him knowing that you would think that Mitch would have more sympathy for my situation but he didn't because he wanted a baby more than anything in the world.

## How Much Can a Soul Take

Tammy T. Cross

This time I think I may be able to carry to the full term since I am not stressed like the last couple of times. Mitch wants me to believe he started cheating after I lost the babies but I know that while I was pregnant that he had been sleeping with someone else a few months into my pregnancy. I just kept it to myself until I caught him in the act but he was smart enough to cover his tracks.

.I remember just like it was yesterday even the conversation that was had, it happened just like this. *I was sitting on the couch waiting for my husband to come home. I had fixed a dinner fit for a king and I was watching a good movie while rubbing my hand across my belly. I did that because I could feel the baby beginning to move and I thought it calmed him down. Yes, I was far enough to know the sex of the baby.*

*Anyways I was sitting there when I got a call from a private number. I usually don't answer but for some odd reason, I did this time. When I answered I heard an unfamiliar voice on the other end of the phone saying, "Hello may I speak to Shay."*

*"This is she may I ask who's calling?" I asked looking at the receiver trying to figure out who she could be and what was she calling me for.*

*"That you don't need to know. All you need to know is don't wait up for your little hubby tonight because he will be with me for a while tonight and when I get done with him I will send*

him home to you." The voice from the other end of the phone informed me.

"Uhmm excuse me but what did you just say and another thing how did you get my number and why are you calling me?" I asked her now sitting up on the couch with steam coming from my ears.

"I got it out of our man's phone when I worked him over and put him to sleep. Would you like for me to wake him up so you can talk to him? Nah I think I will let him sleep for round two then he can come home to you." The young lady said before she hung the phone up in my face.

When she was hanging up the phone up I could hear her laughing on the other end of the receiver. I was so upset I walked through the house tearing the place up. I guess I must have wasted something on the floor that made it slippery because the next thing I knew I went sliding across the floor on my stomach.

When I saw blood I went into a panic mode and I crawled over to the couch grabbed my phone and called 911. When I made it to the hospital I learned that I had cut my hand on a piece of metal that was sticking out from the side of the dishwasher. When the doctor came in he took my vitals and said that my blood pressure was extremely high.

## How Much Can a Soul Take

Tammy T. Cross

Mitch came running through the door because the nurse got his number from my paperwork and informed him I was there. When he came in and grabbed my hand I pulled it away and screamed: "don't touch me, you cheater."

"What are you talking about Shay?" He asked me looking confused.

"Don't play with me Mitchell Bradley I know you been cheating," I shouted out to him.

"Shay, it's just your hormones talking. I am not cheating baby." He said before the doctor stepped in and asked him to leave because my blood pressure was so high now that I was in danger of having a stroke and causing danger to the baby.

I stayed in the hospital for a couple of days before I was able to go home, but while I was there I didn't want to look at Mitchell so I wouldn't let him come to see me. I wanted my blood pressure to regulate so that I could go home. With him there I know it wouldn't be safe for me nor my child.

The day I was released Mitchell came to pick me up from the hospital I rode in silence all the way home. I never even brought up the lady that called me to this day. I decided I would try to catch him so he couldn't deny the fact that he was cheating but he was smart enough to lay low for a while to try and cover his dirt.

## How Much Can a Soul Take

*Tammy T. Cross*

*About a month later I was home cooking dinner and I felt something wet running down my legs. I had a short sundress so it was easy for me to pull it up to see that it was blood. I was only six and a half months pregnant so I knew something had to have been wrong I called the paramedics and they rushed right over and took me to Scott and White Medical Center.*

*When I got there they rushed me into a room and the doctor came in and worked on me for a half hour before he delivered the bad news to me. "I am sorry Mrs. Bradley but you just had a miscarriage, he said and before he exited the room.*

*Everything he said after that was just like the little boy in the movie "Fat Albert" that no one can understand but the gang. That was me I missed every single thing he had to say. I guess in the process I had fainted because when I looked up Mitchell was standing over me rubbing my head in tears.*

*I looked up at him and turned my head. I felt like all of this was his fault. If he wouldn't have been out there messing around I wouldn't have fallen and had this problem in the first place. The thing that hurt me the most is when the doctor told me about the injury I sustained there was a 50/50 chance I could have more children. That was the moment I broke down.*

*After being in the hospital for a few hours the nurse cleaned me up and I was able to go home. For months I didn't say* much of anything to Mitchell. I was hurt to the core and nothing was easing my pain. That is the day I started filling my bar with liquor and easing away from the church. I didn't want to hear anything about the Lord.

My job gave me as much time as I needed off to recover. I stayed off for about three weeks and decided it was time I suck it up and get back to work. Mitch knew he was in the dog house so would come home every night like he was supposed to and played his part in the marriage like he should have in the first place. Five months had passed and I kind of forgave him and ended up trying for another baby.

After a few tries, I ended up pregnant again this time only making it to three months before I miscarried. Once again Mitchell wasn't coming home on time and back to his old tricks. I began to stress and that's what caused me to lose the baby. This time he blamed me but I blamed him because he was repeating the same acts that caused the first miscarriage.

After this loss, he really stopped coming in at night and when he did he was too tired for me. I knew my marriage was over this time. I started praying and asking God to help me and my husband work our relationship out. I asked the Lord what I did that was so bad to deserve this. I always tried to be the best wife *that I could be. It seemed that my prayers were going unanswered until this very moment.*

My husband and I hadn't eaten breakfast together in a long time. I felt like a kid in the candy store as I picked up our plates to clean the kitchen. I was so tired from last night that I barely finished putting the dishes in the dishwasher and wiping down everything. I hurried to my room and slid right back under the cover for a few hours more.

# *Brent*

When my wife and I got up it was the next morning. I woke up an hour before she did. After taking care of my hygiene I went to go check on my son. He was lying on the floor covered with his favorite horse blanket fast asleep. I went into the living room grabbed my key off of the coffee table where I dropped them last night and drove over to Denny's to grab us some breakfast.

Thirty minutes later I came back through the door Jenny and Jaylon were sitting on the couch watching cartoons. Jaylon looked up and saw me walking through the door and shouted, "Daddy! I was wondering where you went."

"Hey, little man daddy went to go and get us some breakfast you and mommy come and join me at the table. We are going to have breakfast as a family today." I told him as I admired the smile that spread across my wife's face.

As we sat down at the table we all grabbed hands and I said the blessing over our food before we gobbled it all down. I looked at my wife and asked, "Honey do you have to go to work today."

"Yes, babe but only for a half of a day. I have some paperwork I have to complete and then I am free. Why what do you have planned?" she looked at me and asked.

"Well, I was hoping you had the whole day off I wanted to get out of town for a while and just spend the day doing something as a family but maybe next time. Us boys will find something to do ain't that right son?" I said reaching over and tickling his armpit trying not to show my disappointment.

"Right daddy," Jaylon shouted with a smile wider than the ocean.

"Well I was going to wait to tell you two but in a couple of weeks, we are going to fly out to Texas for a family reunion. I wanted to surprise you guys but your daddy looks so sad I thought it was best to go ahead and tell you guys the news now." Jenny said looking at me hoping that I would agree to go.

"That's great Jaylon needs to go and see some of his family. Some of them he's never met. He needs to meet them now so he doesn't end up marrying one of them later." I said in a jokingly way.

"You are joking Brent but you do have a point. I am glad you agree because I really wanted you to join me. I waited on purpose because I didn't think you would want to go. I know how much you hated that place. That's the reason we never moved back there anyway," she told me and honestly, she was right.

When I left Bryan I promised myself I would never move back that way. All of my friends ending up getting killed or out on the street making that easy money. I never wanted to live that kind of life because that's the reason my mom wasn't with my dad when I was growing up. He wanted to make that fast money and she wanted to protect me from anyone come to harm me or her because of his street life.

I felt like staying away from that environment would make me a better man and I was right. I am proud to be the man I am today, a man that has a wonderful family. Well, an almost wonderful family that needs a little work. I want to be able to teach my son how to grow up and be a responsible young man. I know without a doubt his mom and I have already done well so far.

"Thanks for breakfast babe but I have to be getting to the office," Jenny said getting up from the table packing our food container over to the trash. She walked into the bathroom washed her hands to remove some of the stickiness from the syrup and washed her face. She then walked out gave Jaylon and I a hug and a kiss before heading out the door for work.

"Jaylon go clean your hands and meet me back in the living room in few minutes and we can watch television for a little while," I told Jaylon walking back in the living room from washing my hands.

"Yes, Sir" Jaylon replied and hurried out of the room.

We sat around until noon watching television until the both of us was tired of sitting in the house. I told him to go put on his shoes I was going to take him to the park to play for a little while. Jaylon ran in the room slid on his shoes and picked up his basketball and we were off.

When we got there he spotted a few friends from school and they hooked up and started to play together. I found a table near the spot he was playing so I could have a seat and watch him play. I know Jenny and I were trying to get back on the right track but Shay was still flooding my mind. I know the Pastor told me I was wrong but it was something about her that I wished I could see in Jenny.

Don't get me wrong she is an incredible woman but Shay is more of a woman than Jenny in so many ways. Shay wants a family and Jenny has one but doesn't really know how to handle one. Shay wants a real man and Jenny is pushing hers away. Shay knows what's she wants out of life and yes Jenny has a good career but money isn't everything. I feel my wife is just working to stay away from us.

Minutes later the Pastor's words came rushing back to me as if he was standing over me warning me to stay away from Shay. My wife and I are trying to work things out and I am finally enjoying spending time with her once again. I shook my head to remove the thoughts of Shay. I noticed that my son was swinging alone and the rest of the kids were gone.

I stood up walked over to the swing and sat in the empty swing beside him. "Dad, I been calling your name for the longest, you didn't hear me?' Jaylon asked as I pushed myself back into the swing to get it going.

"I'm sorry son, I had something on my mind and I must have been lost in thought," I said as I begin to swing a little higher.

"Are you and mommy fighting again dad? I hate it when you two fight it makes me so sad." My son blurted out and put his head down as if to cry.

I dropped my legs really fast and pushed them hard against the ground to stop my swing. I stood up and grabbed his swing to stop his. I then kneeled down in front of him and said, "No Jaylon. I was thinking about something else I had going on but it's nothing for you to be worried about son."

I looked into his eyes and saw that he had the saddest look ever and it crushed my heart. "I am sorry son I never meant to hurt you. Your mother and I may have our differences but it has nothing to do with you. We love you so much Jaylon"

"I know you do daddy but I want you guys to get along so we can be one happy family. Like we use to be before", replied Jaylon as he began to cry.

"Don't cry son you are going to make daddy cry. I promise I will never act like we did the other day again. I love your mother and we are going to be ok. So dry your eyes and let's see who can go the highest in the swing." I said jumping in my swing to try and swing higher than him. He started laughing and before I could get started he was swinging high as the swing could go.

We swung for thirty minutes longer and decided we would leave and go get an ice cream cone before we headed home. We raced to the truck and I let him beat me like always. We got in the truck and drove over to Dairy Queen. The line wasn't long so we made it to the drive-thru window in no time. "I would like to get two chocolate dipped cones please," I told the lady that was working the window.

A few minutes later she returned with two cones and said. "That will be two dollars and fourteen cents sir."

I took the cones and napkins and paid her for the ice cream. We drove home listening to the radio and eating our cones. The song must have gotten good because he was bobbing his head like one of the little bobblehead dolls.

The windows were down and the wind was blowing feeling so good. The words of the song Juju on the beat by Zay Hilfiger and Zayion McCall was getting good to him because he started wiggling in his seat.

*"Walked in this party*
*And these girls lookin' at me*
*Skinny jeans on and you know my hair nappy*
*Hey, hey, hey*
*Okay, okay*
*I want y'all do it, do this dance now*

*JuJu on the beat*
*JuJu on that beat*
*JuJu on that, JuJu on that, JuJu on that beat*
*Now slide, drop*
*Hit dem folks, don't stop, aye*
*Don't stop, aye*
*Don't stop, aye*
*Running man on that beat, aye*
*Running man on that beat, aye*
*Running man on that beat, aye*
*Running man on that beat*
*Now do..."*

Before we could finish the song we were pulling into the driveway and I turned off the engine. "Okay little man that's all you get, it's time to get out and go in the house," I told him as he unbuckled his seatbelt and jump out.

We made our way into the house I sent him to wash up and hang out in his room while I ordered up a pizza from Pizza Hut. I realized Jenny hadn't made it home yet so I looked at my watch and noticed it was way afternoon and she should have been home by now. I then thought to myself her boss must have her working late again like always. The thought of another man flashed through my brain but then I remembered what Pastor Clark said so I left it alone. I grabbed the remote turned the television on and watched Family Feud until our food came.

I guess I had dozed off because I looked up and Jaylon was standing over me saying, "Daddy someone at the door."

"Oh shoot the pizza guy," I shouted running to the door and pulling out my wallet at the same time to pay the guy.

"I am sorry sir I must have fallen to sleep. I didn't hear the doorbell.

"It's ok here is your pizza that will be sixteen dollars and twenty-four cents." The guys replied.

I handed him a twenty and told him to keep the change. He nodded his head and walked away. Jaylon must have been starving because before I could turn around he was sitting at the table with our plates ready to eat. I grabbed us some punch out of the fridge and joined him at the table. When we were done eating he went back in and played his game and I went back to watching TV.

A little while later Jenny came home and gave me the rundown on how her day went. I sat back and listening with a smile on my face. Thinking about how this reminds me of the Jenny I knew when we first met. After we finished our conversation she went and peeked in on Jaylon.

Once she was done the two of us went into our bedroom and got comfortable. We crawled on the bed and popped the movie *"Moonlight"* in the DVD player. We cuddled up under the covers watching our movie until the movie was watching us.

A few weeks had passed by and things were still going great between us. We were now getting ready to take our trip to Texas for Jenny's family reunion. Being that Shay and Jenny were God sister's I didn't know how I was going to act knowing what had happened between the two of us. I couldn't tell Jenny because I knew it would mess up our trip and Jaylon has been packed for it ever since the day his mom told him about.

"Come on you guys the cab is here. I don't want to miss our flight." Jenny yelled out to us and we both came running dragging our bags.

I checked to make sure all of the appliances were turned off and everything was locked up. When I saw that everything was in place I set the alarm and we headed out to the cab. I was so nervous the whole ride to the airport. My hands were all clammy from sweating.

"Are you okay honey you look a little nervous," Jenny asked me waiting for an answer.

"Sure honey it's just you know how I feel about planes. That's why every time I go to Texas I drive." I told Jenny while she laughed at me trying to assure me that everything was going to be alright at the same time.

When we arrived at the airport we went through the checkpoint and loaded our bags and headed to the plane. Once we got to our seats Jaylon was so hyper, he was looking around trying to see what all there was to see. This was the first time he had ever flown on a plane and he was so excited.

When the plane landed, Jenny had a cab drive us over to her mom's house. I don't know why we didn't come the day before the reunion so that we could settle in and get comfortable. I guess because she hated coming back to this place as much as I did.

We pulled up to the house and it was cars everywhere. I paid the cab driver and we climbed out and went in. There were people all over the house and the backyard but the one person I was scared to see was Shay. We walked to Jenny's old room and put up our bags and led Jaylon to the guest room to put his bags up.

When we were all settled we walked out to the backyard and I spotted Shay with her back turned talking to that scum bag husband of hers.

I wanted to run up on him and rip his head off for putting her through so much pain but I didn't want to cause any drama. When he sees me I wonder will he remember me from our high school days. I can't wait to see the look on his face when he looks into my eyes. Then again he was so into chasing women he may not even recognize me. I don't know why I am tripping the past is the past so I guess I need to just chill. I can't help the actions I have always been overprotective of her.

# *Jenny*

I haven't been around my family in God knows when. I came down to this area a few times on a job assignment but no one even knew I was in town. The Lord made my day when he placed Brent in my path years ago. After us trying out a long distance relationship he couldn't handle it any longer and finally moved me to Chicago to be with him. I love my mom but she and I don't see eye to eye from time to time. She is always trying to tell me what I need to be doing and what I need to stop doing and don't nobody want to hear all that.

"So I see you made it Jen, I didn't think you were going to come." My mother said walking up to me calling me by the nickname she gave me years ago. She says it's short for Jenny either way it goes I didn't like it and she knew it. Sometimes I think she did it just to get a reaction out of me but today, it ain't going to work.

"Now mother what would make you think such a thing?" I asked putting my arms around her neck hugging her but deep inside I really wanted to choke her.

"When I called honey you never responded to my call letting me know you if you could make it or not. Anyways you are here and I am glad." She said turning around noticing Brent and Jaylon standing beside me.

"Brent how are you young man it is so nice to see you. I am glad you could make it and how is your mother doing?" She asked Brent as she leaned in to give him a big hug.

"My mother is fine Mama Marie she is always on the go. Right now she is out on a cruise with some of her friends. She says I am grown now she can move around like she wants to." Brent told my mother.

She then smiled and looked down at Jaylon putting her hands over her mouth "Jaylon I haven't seen you in forever." She said reaching down squeezing him tight.

"Hey grandma it is so nice to see you," Jaylon said to my mother.

"Oh, and you are such a respectable young man. Boy come over here and give grandma some sugar." Mama told Jaylon as he moved in and kissed her on her big fluffy cheeks. My mother was a beautiful lady she had long thin hair and her light brown skin was smooth and soft. She was a heavy set lady with big curvy hips. I heard stories that back in the days she was a heartbreaker but she swears that's a myth. She claims to be a Christian but won't own up to being a little on the wild side back in the days.

## How Much Can a Soul Take

*Tammy T. Cross*

She had a great deal of Indian in her blood and you could tell by looking into her face. When I was a kid before my grandmother, my mother's mom, passed away she used to tell me all about the reservation they lived on and how she was so glad to get away and start her family in a place that was safe for her children. Man, I hate she couldn't be here today to see the whole family enjoying the land she worked so hard for them to live easy on.

My mother's house was on one acre out of the four acres of land which was part of the land my grandma owned and passed down to her four children. Now every year they get together on her birthday and throw a big reunion in honor of my grandmother.

I walked around my mother and walked in the direction of Shay calling my name. "Jenny hey sis how are you I haven't seen you in a while. Shay asked hugging me tight as ever.

"I have been good how about you and where is that husband of yours that I never got to meet," I asked not expecting to see the man I saw.

"He ran to the bathroom he will be back shortly. You know how it can be when you have been drinking. When you got to go, you got to go." Shay said smiling big and pretty like she always did.

"Well, you know my husband so it no need in introducing you two," I told Shay looking at her and Brent at the same time.

"Hey Brent, how are you doing?" I am so glad you all could make it and Jaylon boy you are still cute as ever come give your auntie a hug." Shay said reaching down picking Jaylon off the ground and hugging him all at the same time trying not to focus on Brent much.

"Honey come over here and meet my God sister Jenny," Shay said to the man walking up behind us.

I turned around and looked into this man's face I almost past out. Mitchell was the same guy I had met at the restaurant and has been seeing for some time now. When he walked around to give me a hug he was drinking a soda. We came face to face and he almost spits his soda all over me.

"I am sorry ma'am but the acid from the soda went down the wrong pipe and I got choked," Mitchell said to me then held out his hand shaking mine and giving me the side eye all at the same time.

"Hello, my name is Brent, I grew up around here with your wife. It is finally good to meet you. I have heard so much about you. Brent told Mitchell with a mean look on his face.

"Brent why are you looking like that," I asked him beginning to feel nervous hoping he didn't know about Mitchell and me.

"Yes, babe I am fine I just thought that Mitchell here looks a little familiar to me," Brent replied.

"I doubt that you know him. You know they say everyone has a look-alike and that could be it, Brent. Oh and Shay I will talk to you later I am about to take Brent around to greet everyone. I said as we walked off.

"Nice to meet you Brent and Shonda," Mitchell said as Brent and I walked away.

"Who is Shonda, her name is Jenny," Shay said laughing at Mitchell while I gave him the side eye behind her back.

"My bad bae I am sorry, I mean Jenny. Mitchell said sarcastically as we walked away.

When we got across the yard I could see Mitchell eyeing me down with a mean look on his face. Out of all the time we were messing around I never told him I had neither a child nor a husband. If my mother knew all of this was going on I know she would drown me with a whole bottle of holy oil. This is one thing I know she wouldn't agree with.

I sat in the corner with my aunt and uncle for hours trying to avoid Shay and her husband. I was praying she didn't come over here because I would then have to face that husband of hers. Yeah, I knew I was wrong for getting involved with this man and lying about my real name but I never thought I would run into him at a family event. To top it off he is my God sister's husband! Boy, I have really screwed up big time.

"Excuse me Brent but I am about to go to the bathroom and I will be right back," I told him making a dash to the back entrance of the house disappearing inside hoping no one will see me go inside because I needed time to escape from everyone for a moment.

I rushed to the bathroom and let the toilet seat down and sit on it for a minute. Not even a few minutes later I begin to feel a little sick in the stomach. I didn't know if it was because of all of the things that were going on around me or if I was coming down with something. All at once I jumped up and lifted the toilet seat, dropped down on my knees and put my head over the toilet throwing up like crazy.

I thought to myself where did that all come from. I stood up and reached into the cabinet above the sink and got a face towel down and washed my face. I laid the towel down on the side of the sink and started to rinse my mouth out with a little water. The last time I filled my mouth with water I stopped whispered to myself *"this can't be happening. I haven't had a cycle in a while."*

I picked up the towel washed my face one last time and sat back down on the toilet. *"God this can't be happening to me. What am I going to do? Not only could I be pregnant but it's a chance it could be my God sister's husband's baby. Lord I know they say what's done in the dark will come to the light but Lord if you will please get me out of this mess I promise I won't ever do a thing like this again."*

Ten minutes later I heard a knock on the door. I grabbed the towel and washed the tears that were falling down my face away. I know it had to be Brent coming to check up on me. "Give me a minute" I shouted to him.

He must have gotten impatient because the door came flying open but instead of Brent walking in. Mitchell walked in and closed the door behind him. I jumped up and whispered, "Mitchell what are you doing, are you crazy?"

"Why did you lie to me Shonda or whatever your name is? I fell for you and even put my wife through nights of misery because of you. All this time you were just playing me." Mitchell yelled in anger.

"Mitchell I-I- I never…" I tried to explain.

"Save it you got what you wanted from me and ran back to your little happy family and just left me waiting for you to return. Yeah, we talk on the phone all the time and you feed me those sweet lies but never once said anything about a family. I was willing to give everything up for you. I guess it's true the grass isn't always greener on the other side," Mitchell said as he gripped my arm.

"Mitchell let go you're hurting my arm," I said yanking my arm from the grip of his hand.

He looked over at the toilet and notice that I had been throwing up because I had gotten a little onto the floor. What's wrong with you, are you pregnant." He walked over to the toilet and lifted the seat and saw that I had released a load. I didn't even realize that I hadn't flushed it yet.

"No, I am not I just got overheated out there," I told him praying and hoping that was the truth.

"Are you sure because I have been feeling some kind of way lately and each time Shay got pregnant I felt this same feeling." He said and it made my heart skip a beat.

"Look, Mitchell, I have to get back outside if they catch us in here together it is going to be some trouble." I said flushing the toilet and trying to rush out of the bathroom and didn't make it before he grabbed me and start to kiss me."

After a few minutes, I realized what we were doing, was just what I prayed and told God I wouldn't do again. I yanked away and ran out of the bathroom running slap into my mother when I turned the corner.

"Girl what is wrong with you running like someone is after you. My mother said peeking around me trying to see if someone was behind me.

"No mother I thought I heard this certain song playing out back. I was trying to get back outside to hear it. You know I always did love the way Uncle Ray DJ at our reunions." I said grabbing her by the hand trying to lead her back out the door before she saw Mitchell.

"Now girl you know I don't get down with that kind of music no more. Now if he put on some Kirk Franklin I will show you how the Saints get down." Mother said as she started moving around like she was about to shout.

"Oh mama you are a mess come on let's go out here and enjoy the family," I said trying to push her out the door when all of a sudden Mitchell came walking from around the corner.

My mother waited well until he made it outside. "Now, Jenny, I may be old but I ain't crazy. What in the devil you got going on and don't lie to me. I can smell a rat when I see one." She said looking me in my eyes as if the truth was already written on my forehead.

"I grabbed my forehead and said mama it's not what you think," I told her before she cut me off.

Jenny that is your God sister's husband, girl what is wrong with you. Walking around here acting like a lil hussy." She said with the look of disgust written all over her face.

"Mama," was all I managed to get out.

"Don't you mama me I didn't raise you like that," Oh my Gosh and look at you, you got that look written all over your face. The same look you had years ago."

"What are you talking about?" I looked at her with a frown on my face trying to understand what she was saying.

"Jenny are you pregnant?" I can see it all in your face." My mother asked at the same time Brent walked in and stopped in his tracks.

"Hey you two what is going on, babe I came to see what was taking you so long?" Brent asked as I rolled my eyes at my mother and tried to put a smile on my face.

"I think I had gotten a little overheated that's all I was on my way back outside before my mother stopped me. " I told him hoping he did not overhear our conversation.

"Mama Marie can I please talk to Jenny for a minute," Brent asked?

"Sure I will be out back if you guys need me." My mother said eyeing me all the way out the door.

"Baby I overheard your mother saying you were pregnant is that true?" He asked me as he placed his hand on my stomach.

I thought about my prayer to God and decided that I wouldn't lie about me possibly being pregnant. "Yes, Brent there is a chance I may be pregnant."

"Why didn't you tell me, babe. You know I have always wanted another baby." He told me as he dropped to his knees and began to kiss my stomach.

He looked up at me and I was now in tears. Not because I wasn't happy about the baby but because I wasn't sure if this was even his child. Brent stood up and looked at me with a look of confusion. I tried to control my cry but I began to sob even heavier.

"Jenny, what's going on are you saying you don't want to be pregnant?" Brent sadly asked.

"It's not that I think it's just my hormones." I lied and said all while praying to God to forgive me for yet another lie.

"It is going to be fine babe. I am here for you" Brent said as he gently kissed my wet cheeks.

"You go back out there and join the family. I don't feel good I think I am going to go lie down for a little while." I told

Brent as I kissed him back and headed to the bedroom we were going to be staying in while we were visiting.

He agreed that I needed some rest and went back outside to hang out with the family. I went into the bedroom this time locking the door behind me. I didn't want any more surprises. I walked into the bathroom that was connected to the room and ran me a nice bubble bath. I climbed in and took a long bath.

Forty-five minutes later I got out dried myself off and slid on my favorite Mickey Mouse pajamas. I walked over to the bed pulled the covers back and slid in. I rolled over to the window and pulled the sham back just a little so that I could look out over the backyard at everyone having a good time.

My mother was sitting on the opposite side of the yard watching every move Mitchell made. I tell you when my mother had a feeling about something there is nothing no one can say or do to change the way she feels. Truth is nine times out of ten that woman was always right.

Mitchell, on the other hand, has been looking around the yard as if he was looking for me. Shay was all over the place like always talking to everyone. That is the way she has always been a girl with a good heart but never knew how to pick the right guy. I can see that because the man she married is just as foul as the other guys she dated when she was younger.

I pushed the curtain closed and just laid around deep in thought. I was disturbed by the knock on the door. I jumped up and looked at the door scared to open it. "Who is it?" I shouted from the inside of the door.

"It's me bae let me in," Brent shouted from the other side of the door.

I opened the door and let him and Jaylon in. Jaylon was bouncing off the wall from all of the sweets he had eaten. I didn't have to see him to know because this is how he acted every single time he eats a lot of sweets.

"Mommy you missed everything we had so much fun. I danced with Uncle Ray and he taught me a new line dance. I don't know the name of it but I can show you how it goes." Jaylon said jumping off the bed dancing across the floor.

'Wow look at you little man. You will have to teach me that later. I see daddy got you all cleaned up and you can play your game until you ready for bed. Your daddy can go help you hook up your game." I told him as I lay back down on the bed.

"Daddy already helped me I just came in here to tell you good night daddy said you weren't feeling good and I wanted to give you a kiss and make you all better," Jaylon said as he leaned in and kissed my cheek and bounced right on to the guest bedroom.

Brent closed the door behind him and dug through the duffle bag and grabbed his pajamas out to go take a shower. "Hey, Jenny Shay told me to tell you she hopes you feel better and Mitchell said to tell Shonda it was nice to meet her. I laughed and said you mean Jenny." He told me as he chuckled and went into the bathroom to go shower.

I threw on a fake smile until he went into the bathroom. I wanted to shoot Mitchell a text and let him know that my mother was on to him and to stay away from me but I decided I would just leave it alone. I rolled back over in the bed and pulled the covers up to my neck. My mother had it so cold in the house I was starting to freeze. A little while later Brent was joining me in bed we cuddled up close and he talked about all of the things that happened today for hours.

# *Mitchell*

"Hey, handsome did you miss me? I may be in your area soon but I am not really sure yet," Shonda asked before I could get hello out good.

"Yes I did I can't wait for you to come back I have something I want to talk to you about," I told her.

"Oh yeah should I be worried' she started to asked me before I heard another voice talking to her in the background and she told me she would call me back.

I waited a week and she never called me back. Then a month went by and I still hadn't heard from her. I was starting to think she had blown me off so I fought even harder to fix me and Shay's relationship. We even started to work on having a baby. I prayed that the Lord bless us with one that makes it to full term this time.

When my wife told me we were going to her family reunion I was excited. I could now finally meet some of her family that I have never met before. I also want to meet this God sister that she is always talking about. I want to tell her just how much Shay been missing her.

"Hey, baby you ready to go I don't want to be late. I want to get there and find a good place to park. Even though it is a full four acres out there I want to park as close to the house as possible you know I hate walking far." Shay told me while grabbing her purse walking toward the door.

"I looked at her and laughed and said, "Come on here girl lets go. It ain't going to hurt your little butt if you have to walk a little bit."

"Boy who you fooling you know a lil fine thang like me can't be sweating." She giggled and said as we got into the car and drove over to her God mother's house.

We made it there, we hurried up and got out and went in. "Hey Godmother Marie this is my husband Mitchell," Shay said introducing me.

"Heyyy Mitchell, you are a handsome young man. Shay, you have done well for yourself." Her Godmother said as she stood there checking me out.

She led us into the house and out to the backyard where the rest of the family were all out laughing, dancing and having a good time. Shay then took me around and introduces me to the other family members when all of a sudden Jenny walked up to us hugging Shay. I could have chocked the life out of her.

I looked at her with anger in my eyes because all along I been meeting up with her thinking she was a woman named Shonda. To top it off she is Shay's God sister and has a family. What kind of stunt is this woman pulling? Whenever I get a chance I am going to find out just what she got going on. I mean I was falling in love with this woman and now I see why I haven't heard from her.

After I saw Jenny go into the house I waited a while and told Shay. "I am going to go inside and go to the bathroom."

"Okay, Mitch when you go into the kitchen go toward the living room until you reach the hallway and make a right the bathroom is at the end of the hall." She told me before she turns around and started back talking to one of her cousins that just had walked up.

I stood at the door I could hear the water running. A few minutes later I could have sworn I heard crying. I knocked on the door and when I heard her voice I just barged in. Lucky the door was unlocked and I didn't have to break in. I walked in and went straight off on her.

When I saw that she had been throwing up. I looked at her and noticed she had picked up a few pounds from the last time I saw her. When I asked her was she pregnant and she made her way out of the bathroom I just stood there not knowing if I should be shocked or happy to finally be a dad. I then said to myself, "Okay nut this woman has pulled so many tricks. How do you even know this is even your baby?"

I pushed the bathroom door shut until I felt the coast was clear. At least I thought it was clear until I ran into her and her mother standing in the kitchen going at it about something. I eased on out the back door and sat next to Shay until it was time to go. The way her Godmother was eyeing me I didn't want to cause a disturbance. I could tell she was on to something and I just sat back and tried to act natural.

I was so glad this reunion was over and we had just made it home. Yeah, I had a great time but I was more focused on what I just learned today about this so-called woman I thought I knew. Shay and I went and got cleaned up and put on our bedclothes. When we got in the bed Shay was so tired she went right to sleep.

I tossed and turned all night thinking about Shonda, Jenny or whatever her name is. How am I going to tell Shay if this is my baby? This will crush her knowing how hard it was for her to become pregnant and to lose not one but two babies.

*"Lord I know I haven't talked to you in a while and I may be the last person you want to hear from but I need you to help me*

*fix this right now. Women are my weakness and this time I think I overstepped my boundaries. My mother always told me growing up "you may run from God but he will find a way to make you run back to him" and Lord I guess she was right.*

*I want to do right by my wife. I no longer want to put her through any pain I just need you to work this out for my good. I promise I will be done with my doggish ways if you bring me out of this one. Amen."*

As hard as it may be I am going to let Jenny be with her husband. They look so happy together and I don't want to tear their family apart. They have a son that needs them more than I need Jenny. I have to admit that woman had me tied around her finger and it's going to be hard not being with her but if I want the Lord to help me I am going to have to stay in my lane.

Shay rolled over and I was still awake, "Baby why you not sleep?" She asked me.

"I was watching you sleep beautifully." I told her wrapping my arms around her and pulling her in close. She snuggled up in my chest and we both eventually drifted off to sleep.

The next morning she was up and already had breakfast ready when I walked in the room. I snuck up behind her as she was setting the table and kissed her on the cheek. "Mitch you scared me. Good morning sit down let me fix your plate."

When she finished fixing our plates she poured us a glass of orange juice and joined me at the table. I took a bit of my bacon and it hit the spot. "I had a really nice time at the reunion yesterday babe and your family is really nice," I told her getting a conversation started.

"It was nice and I so enjoyed myself. I was beginning to think you weren't having a good time after a while. The vibe I got from you when you came back from the bathroom was different than before." She told me looking as if she was waiting for an answer.

"No I was fine but the heat was getting to me. You know my sexy self-doesn't take heat to well." I joked trying to mimic her from our conversation about the heat yesterday.

It must have worked because she laughed and threw a napkin at me and said, "Really Mitch, finish up so we can make it to church on time. Oh and all of the family will be there today. We want to spend time together at church before everyone says goodbye and go back home."

I took a big swig of my orange juice, stood up taking my plate to the kitchen and headed to the room to get dressed. I didn't want her to see the expression on my face right now. I really didn't want to go but I put on my best Sunday clothes and waited for her to finish so we could leave and get this over with. "Okay baby lets go." She said as she walked in with her keys in her hand and her purse hanging from her right shoulder.

We drove over to the church which we haven't been to together as a couple in a while. We found an empty seat right behind Jenny and Brent. When we sat down Brent turned around and said hello while Jenny pretended she was into the message Pastor Rockwell was speaking. Brent then tapped her on the shoulder to tell her we were there and she glanced around waved and turned back around quickly.

Man the message that the Pastor preached today was one I will never forget. He said, *"there are some of you that are walking around here with a few skeletons in your closet. I advise you to get it right. Y'all do know that God is coming back but the question is will you be ready. We got men running around her sleeping with women acting like some dogs in heat. Women, you are not excused you all are running around messing with married men acting like y'all proud to be a side piece.*

*Now, do you think that man going to make you their main chick when he got a whole woman at home that he is committed to? Honey, he's just telling you what you want to hear just to get to the fountain of youth between your legs. You all better start praying and asking God to send you a man of your own. It's too much going on around here to be sleeping with every Tom, Dick, and Harry.*

*My children of God I know this may have ruffled some of your features today but I wouldn't be a servant of God if I didn't tell you what God has led me to tell you. I struggled with this message when God gave it to me but I said God please help me to say it in a way that I can reach your people without coming off like I am judging them.*

*Either way, it goes if I did hurt some feelings I can't be worried about that. I just pray you all get it right and soon because God is on his way back and I pray that you all are ready."* He then grabbed his bible and walked into his office while the deacon stood up and closed out the service.

When church was over we all met up outside of the church and said our goodbyes. I hugged Shay's Godmother and was about to walk away when Shay said she had something to share with everyone.

"Before we all go I would like to share something with you all. I had been feeling sick and I went to the doctor on Friday and found out that I am pregnant." Shay blurted out and I couldn't show my excitement because of the fact that Jenny was pregnant too and that could possibly be my baby too.

"Well join the club Shay, Jenny is expecting to, aren't you Jenny." Shay's Godmother said looking at me and Jenny as if she knew something had been going on with her daughter and me.

"Mama Brent and I weren't saying anything yet because we haven't been to the doctor yet," Jenny shouted angrily.

"Oh ok tell me this, when was the last time your black behind had your cycle." That's what I thought. Don't get quite now keep talking and tell them the truth." Jenny mother said stepping up like she was waiting for her to say one word.

Jenny told everyone goodbye, grabbed Brent and Jaylon and told them to come on so they could catch their flight. Everyone else stood back and watched the hurried away in the rental car she rented headed from Easterwood Airport. After they left we all went our separate ways.

When we made it home I was feeling the excitement kicking in knowing my wife was pregnant once again. I grabbed her purse and pulled off of her shoes and rubbed her feet. I didn't want her cooking so I ordered Chinese food and we sat in the living room eating and chatting away. This time around I promised my wife I was going to be the best husband a man could be and I mean every word of it.

# Shay

Ever since I revealed to my husband that I was pregnant he has been catering to my every need. He even got off work early just to fix dinner for me. I tried to assure him that I am okay to cook but he said he wanted me off of my feet every chance I get. I have to admit I was enjoying this.

Some time has passed and it was time for me to go to my next doctor's appointment and Mitchell took off to go with me. I was far enough now where I was able to find out the sex of the baby. Yea I kept this from him a while because I want to make sure things were going well with this pregnancy. After my last visit to the doctor, he told me that everything looked great and from the looks of it this baby is going to make it into the world this time.

"Mr. and Mrs. Bradley are you two ready to find out what you guys are going to have." The nurse asked as she squeezed that cold blue gel onto my stomach and started rubbing a little thing that looks like a wand over my stomach.

I looked at Mitch and he looked at me. We smiled at the nurse and nodded our heads while looking out our little baby's heartbeat on the monitor." Looks like you guys will be having a baby girl.' The nurse said looking at Mitchell to see if he was as happy as I was.

Mitchell didn't care what the sex was, just as long as it was a healthy baby. He had so much excitement in his eyes. Looking at my husband I think he was happier than me. On our way home we stopped by several different stores and looked at baby stuff. Now that we know the sex he not only looked at stuff he picked up

*Tammy T. Cross*

a few items too. He said they were too cute to pass up and his baby girl just had to have them.

I can't wait until these next few months pass because I don't know how much more I could take of this man being so overprotective of me. I kind of understand why he is acting like this but I am to close now to lose this baby. I prayed to God that he blessed me to see this baby make it into the world. I am a true believer that he will do just what I ask of him. Now that I have been including God into everything that I am doing my life has changed tremendously. I know there will be some hard times that will arise but I know that God will bring me through that to.

Mitchell and I got back into church like we should have been all along. We haven't been fighting and his cheating ways were long gone. Don't get me wrong we have our days that we have disagreements but what couple doesn't. I can say it doesn't last long we normally come to an agreement very quickly.

Months have passed by and the doctor said that the baby could come any day now. I was at home on maternity leave when I was walking to the washer to put in a load of clothes. I started feeling something wet on my legs and I started crying because it was the same feeling I felt the day I lost my last baby. I had a strap around my waist that held my cell phone just for days like this.

*Tammy T. Cross*

I made my way to the front door and unlocked it. Then I wobbled to the couch and dialed 911. "Hello this is Shay Bradley I live at 213 West Summer Street, can you please send an ambulance I think something is wrong. I am pregnant and it's water running down my legs."

"Stay on the phone ma'am I think you are in labor how far along are you?" The woman on the other end of the phone asked me.

I began to breathe hard because the pain was now kicking in. After I got my breaths in I managed to say "I am nine months. "Then I screamed out because the pain I just felt was becoming unbearable.

All at once it was as Mitchell could feel that something was wrong because he came running through the door. He ran in so fast I could have sworn I felt the wind from it when he swung it open. He was shaking more than me and I am the one having a baby. "I called the ambulance and they are on their way. They were taking so long I couldn't hold it any longer I have to push.

Mitchell jumped up ran to the room and grabbed a blanket. I don't know how he did it but he managed to put it under me to prevent me from messing up the couch. As soon as he got it under me he propped my legs up on the couch snatched my underwear

94 | P a g e

off from under my dress and when I pushed he caught the baby right before she hit the floor.

He stood there holding her like he couldn't believe that this was really happening. My husband just had delivered his first baby girl. Moments later the paramedics rushed in and checked me and the baby out. "Ma'am you look great and so does the baby let us get you two over to the hospital." The guy said as he loaded the baby and me onto the stretcher.

Mitchell went into the room and grabbed our hospital bags that I have had packed for months. He got in the car and followed us over to the hospital. When we made it there they took me to a room where they cleaned me up and hooked me to an IV. I was so tired that I could hardly keep my eyes open. Mitch told me to get some rest he would keep an eye on the baby. I couldn't take it any longer as soon as my head went back on the pillow I was out.

*Tammy T. Cross*

# Brent

Ever since we got home Jenny's been acting some kind of way. I don't know if it was because her mom revealed to everyone that she was pregnant or it has something to do with Mitchell. I tell you the looks and the vibe I got from the two of them was getting to me. They can fool everyone else but they weren't fooling me.

I had been trying to be romantic with her like we were before we went to Texas. She, on the other hand, kept pushing me away. I wanted to pick up the phone and talk to Shay because she always understood me but I didn't think that was wise since we crossed the line. Also with her being pregnant, I didn't want to stress her out. That's what caused her to lose her first two babies.

I tried to give Jenny a little space because I know how women that become pregnant can have different mood swings. She started coming home from work every day going straight to her room. Jaylon and I had to fend for ourselves when it came to dinner. My job as a car salesman didn't allow me to work long hours like Jenny. That allows me to be able to spend more time with our son.

A month after us been home from our visit to Texas I came home from work early and Jenny was already home. I step out of my truck and felt the hood of her car and it was cold so that meant she had to have been home for a while. I walked into the house and into the bedroom where she was lying across the bed like something was wrong with her.

"Jenny are you okay" I yelled pulling the cover back off of her limp body. There was blood everywhere I pulled my cell phone out of my pocket and called 911. "Can you guys please send someone I walked in the house and my wife is lying across the bed and its blood everywhere? Can you please hurry she is pregnant. We leave at 5213 Prentice Lane." I shouted to the operator that was on the phone.

Ten minutes later they were pulling up to the house and I went to the door and let them in. I showed them to the bedroom where my wife was laying as if she was in shock. When the guy went to check her out he informed me that she had just had a miscarriage. I broke down because I was looking forward to having a newborn around as well as being a new daddy.

I gathered her some more clothes for her to change into when she was released and set it up where Jaylon could leave from school and go home with Mrs. Jackson one of Jaylon best friend's mother. I drove fast all the way over to the hospital. When I got there Jenny was already settled in a room. She was lying there with her head facing the window with a sad look on her face.

I knocked on the door and walked in. I sat down on the side of her bed rubbing my fingers through her hair. "Hey, beautiful how are you feeling?" I ask her.

She looked at me and turned her head to the other side. "How do you think I feel I just lost a baby?" She snapped at me as if it was my fault.

"Hold on baby I am here to check on you. I am your husband and that was my baby, I care about you." I told her as I stood up looking down at her.

"Tah huh, you thought" she mumble but it wasn't low enough that I didn't understand her.

'What did you just say Jenny. So you are telling me that wasn't my baby. Is that what you are saying J?" That's what I call her when I get upset with her.

"No Brent it wasn't, it was Mitchell's baby. My God sister's husband, I was slipping off to Texas to be with him when you thought I was working." Jenny yelled out so loud the nurse came running.

"How could you do Shay like that Jenny? I hope you don't plan on telling her this. She doesn't need the stress this could make her lose her baby." I told her standing there giving her an angry look.

"Don't worry I don't plan on telling your girlfriend about Mitch and I. Besides I was never introduced to Mitchell before the reunion so I was unaware he was her husband." She blurted out.

"Girlfriend, Jenny what do you mean? Shay is just a friend." I replied.

"Save it, Brent, you can't deny it. You were in the shower one day and I looked at your phone and seen the text she sent you about how you guys shouldn't have done what y'all did and it couldn't happen anymore." Jenny said leaving me speechless.

All I could do was walk out of the room and sit in the lobby and think for a while. I should be mad but I really can't say much because I slept with Shay. I only messed with Shay once and we used protection so I know that baby she is carrying is not mine but I am so upset that Jenny could be so careless. I pulled myself together and went back to Jenny's room.

The doctor came back in and told Jenny she was fine and could go home. She lost her baby but she didn't damage anything. I handed her the clothes I picked out for her to put on. They brought her discharge paper into the room and wheelchair and we were out the door and on our way home.

The whole ride home neither one of us said a word to each other. When we arrived home and went inside I called Mrs. Jones and ask her could Jaylon stay the night and I will pick him up in the morning. "No problem Brent" She gladly told me.

Jenny walks straight to the room slamming the door behind her. She then walked back out and threw a pillow and a blanket on the couch for me. I looked at her like she was crazy but I didn't say a word I think it's best for me to sleep on the couch anyways.

The next morning I picked up the phone and called my Pastor and talked to him about what all has been going on. "Brent you and Jenny got a mess going on over there. Give me a little bit of time I will come over and talk to you both." He told me hanging up.

I had so much on my mind I forgot I had to go pick up Jaylon. Mrs. Jones called and told me if I needed more time Jaylon would be fine there with her. I told her yes I did and thanked for being some helpful. I hung up the phone and the Pastor was already at the door.

"Come on in Pastor, you made it faster than I expected," I told him.

I had another stop to make but the Lord showed me that could wait and this was more important. Now, where is Jenny?" Pastor Clark asked.

I pointed toward the room. Good as he felt he walked over and knocked on the door and yelled in the room for Jenny to come out. It took her a few minutes but she strolled in like a half-dead woman. "How are you feeling Jenny," Pastor Clark asked?

"I could be better," she dragged out.

"Look, I am not going to drag this on a long time but I know what's been going on with you and Brent and that's why I am here." Pastor Clack expressed.

"I don't mean to be rude but I really don't feel like dealing with this right now," Jenny said.

"I understand that baby but I am here and we are going to clear this mess up and now" He shouted in a strong and stern voice.

"Yes, Sir" Jenny responded.

"Now like I told Brent when I talk to him a few months back neither one of you guys have room to be mad at one another. The both of y'all been jumping from bed to bed with someone else so Jenny how could you be mad and Brent you don't have that right either and you already know that." He told us as we sat and listened.

"Jenny you were out spreading your love with a man and weren't protecting yourself and then got pregnant. Baby, I know this man loves you because any other man would have beaten you down or left you here alone. Thank the Lord none of that happened." He said spitting nothing but the truth. Lord knows I wanted to snatch her out that bed talking to me like she did.

Jenny began to cry and I hated to see her cry. I got up and sat behind her and wrapped her in my arms. "You guys got a son to raise, y'all don't want your son to be out there running from woman to woman. You guys have to get yourself together so you can make him a better person. A child learns from what he sees his parents do." The Pastor said and it struck a nerve for the both of us.

"You are right and even though it hurt that she messed around and got pregnant I forgive her. I love my wife no matter what. Some people may say a man like me is weak but I have my faults too and I want to be forgiven." I told the Pastor.

"Brent I forgive you also and I was so hurt that I lost my baby that I took it out on you. I have to tell you one more thing." Jenny told me and I was wondering if I could handle any more news from her.

"I hope you aren't trying to hurt Brent anymore." The Pastor started saying when she cut him off.

"No listen, both of you, the baby was your's, Brent. If you would have noticed how far along I was you would have known. I hadn't been on a trip for work in a while. I was three and a half weeks pregnant. It had been two months since I visited Texas last." Jenny admitted.

Knowing that this baby was really mine made me weak in my knees I wanted to cry my heart out but I was trying to be strong for my wife. I leaned in and pulled her even closer to me. My heart was hurting for her because she was the one that was carrying the baby and to just lose something that she had grown attached to even if she hadn't seen it yet, it still could be devastating.

"We want to thank you for stopping by Pastor, you always did know how to make things right when Jenny and I were having hard times," I told him as I stood up and shook his hand.

Let me pray for you two before I go. *"Father God I ask that you come into this house and remove the demons that are trying to tear this family apart. Lord, you know everything that has transpired in their lives and I ask you to remove the negative things that are surrounding the two of them. Lord they love one another and the devil wants to see them fight but you are a God of love and I ask that you step in and remove all of Satan's evil tactics right this moment. I know it won't be easy for them to fully forgive right now but I ask you to give them a forgiving heart so they can make this marriage and family complete once again. In Jesus name Amen.*

I stood up and walked him to the door. I turned around and led my wife back to the bedroom and helped her finish cleaning up the bed which she had started doing before the Pastor came. I was tired and so was she so we both climbed into bed to rest. I laid there and held her for hours. I couldn't help but think about the baby and I cried as Jenny slept her pain away.

I eased up and let her sleep and drove over to Mrs. Jones house to pick up Jaylon. He had already eaten at her house so I didn't have to stop and get him anything to eat. I wasn't hungry they way I was feeling made me not have an appetite. I lay on the couch and watched television for the rest of the night while Jaylon went to his room.

It took us a while but after a few months, things started to get back on track for us. My wife and I were doing more things together and spending a lot of time doing things with Jaylon. The loss of our baby hurt us so badly that we decided that we would wait a while before we tried again. We got back into the church and were very active in the church. We were helping out with anything that was needed at the church.

Jaylon had gotten to the point that his grades started slipping because of the problems we were having at home. We all started going to counseling to help work on how to deal with all of the problems because even after talking to the Pastor we still had issues from time to time. This helped tremendously, Jaylon is now doing well in school and our family is doing so much better. At this moment I couldn't ask God to bless my family any other way.

# Shay

I was so happy to finally wake up to see my beautiful baby girl. Mitchell was so happy he stayed at the nursery the whole time they cleaned her up. Once they were done and she was able to come from under the warmer he had the nurse bring her to the room so that he could look at her while I rested.

Mitch has heard so much about babies being stolen from the nursery that he vowed he was keeping his eye on the baby every chance he got. I told him that they have alarms on the baby's foot now and that she was going to be just fine. Lord, I can see now that I am going to have one spoiled baby and it won't be me that's going to be doing the spoiling.

I was so excited that I had a healthy baby that I hadn't even taken time out to name her yet. Mitchell and I both agreed to name her Mackenzie LaShay Bradley. The lady came in and we filled out all the paperwork for her name and for her birth certificate. I looked at Mitchell and said, "they do not be playing, they rush in here on you with all this paperwork at one time."

It was getting late and Mitchell didn't want to stay the night at the hospital because he wanted me to get some sleep. He went home to get him some rest and to bring back the car seat which he had forgotten to load up in the car when the paramedics brought me in.

After he left I called my family to let them know that I had the baby and when I talked to my Godmother she informed me that Jenny had lost her baby and she was depressed but is doing so much better now. She said, "Shay they got back in church and I am so happy for them."

'That is so good, Mitchell and I have gotten back into the church to and our relationship has been so much better," I told my Godmother.

"Baby, when you have God in your life all things, works for your good. I tell you without Him I don't know where I would be today" She told me.

"That is so true mama I can't believe the things He has done for me but I know it's late and before we start having church. I am going to get off the phone now. I love you," I told her as I hung up the phone because I could feel myself getting overjoyed.

After hanging up the phone I called the nurse back in to take my baby down to the nursery. I then turned over and went back to sleep. I was in and out of sleep all night with the nurses messing with me I couldn't wait until it was time for me to go home to get a good night's rest.

After staying a couple of nights in the hospital, I was able to go home. Mitchell came in and helped the nurse load us up in the car. He hooked Mackenzie up and we were on our way home. We made it home quickly and I was so happy that I hurried inside. When I got in the house I noticed that Mitchell had the baby's bed already put up and everything in order for her. I leaned over and kissed him and said, "Thanks baby for all you have done while we were at the hospital."

"He joked and said, Girl don't kiss me like that anymore that's how we got Mackenzie."

"Boy hush it was just a little kiss. Now she all yours for a little while I need a good nap I couldn't get any sleep at the hospital." I told him as I walked away.

A few weeks have passed and things were close to normal again and Mitchell was coping so well with the baby and I loved every minute of it. He then decided that he didn't want me working anymore and wanted me to be a stay at home mom. I didn't mind it one bit because I didn't want anyone caring for my baby but me. Mitchell was so attached to the baby that every day he came home from work he was all over her.

I was so happy about the relationship he has with the baby and I. A few years back I didn't think that we would ever have a relationship this strong. There was no doubt in my mind that Mitchell didn't love me because he truly did with all of his heart. We may have had our ups and downs but we still knew how to come together and let each other know just how much we meant to each other.

I had friends and family say that he was no good for me and that I needed to leave him but they had to understand that I wasn't making a move until God gave me the okay to move. A few told me that he gave me the okay when he started cheating but they didn't understand the relationship that I had with God.

I had to tell them they could say what God wants me to do but they have to understand that until God gives me that message that's when I will leave. I felt like no one has a perfect relationship and it's up to you to make it work. I knew Mitchell was hurting because he wanted a baby and no cheating wasn't the answer but that was a way I felt he was dealing with the loss of our precious babies.

Mitchell and I still to this day have our rough spots but we have learned to sit down and talk them over. Just like today he had, had a rough day at work and due to the baby being cranky all day I was slow getting dinner ready on time. He came in with an ugly attitude so I laid Mackenzie in her bed and pulled him to the side to talk.

"Look, Mitchell, I don't know what you are going through but I have had a long day with the baby. For some reason, she has been cranky all day." I sat down on the couch next to him and said.

"I am sorry that I came in here snapping at you like I did but I have had a long stressful day and I shouldn't have taken it out on you. How is the baby, do you know what's wrong?" He said while sliding in close to me grabbing me by the hand.

"I am not sure, but I think it's just a little gas. I gave her some gas drops and she seems to be doing a little better. I replied.

"I am glad she is doing better. Is there anything you would like for me to help you do?" He asked feeling bad about the way he came in the door acting.

"No, I am almost done but one thing you can do is the next time you think about coming through that door yelling about me not having dinner ready, you better think twice because you almost made the bad Shay come out on you boy," I said getting up from the couch throwing a plush pillow at him.

"Hey, I said I am sorry now get your fine self in there and fix my dinner woman." He smiled and jokingly said.

Once I finished dinner we sat down to enjoy some good old fried fish, potato salad, hush puppies and a salad. I also made us a pitcher of cherry Kool-Aid. When we began to eat he told me about the problems he had at work today. I could understand why he was upset but I just sit back and lend him a listening ear.

When dinner was over I cleaned the kitchen while Mitchell went to do what he did best and that spoiled our child. I could hear him talking to her and her cooing back at him. That causes me to feel all happy and warm inside. I tell you when he is down that little girl sure knows how to lift his spirits up.

Even though it seemed that things were back to normal, I still find it hard to completely forgive him. I mean I said to myself that I did but then I thought to myself did I really wholeheartedly forgive him? I started having sessions with Pastor Richmond down at Mt. Believers Baptist Church and he taught me how to give all my problems to God and leave them there.

Mitchell and I agreed that whatever happened in the past we would leave it there and start fresh. So since I never told him about my one night stand with Brent I never questioned him about the person he was cheating with. I felt that was more than fair.

As for Brent and I, we only communicated over the phone from time to time. Letting each other know how things were going with our lives but nothing more. He apologized to me several times for what happened between us but I had to let him know I had a part in that too and that as long as we never let it happen again we would be fine.

Brent informed me that he and Jenny still have issues from time to time but nothing so serious they couldn't work it out. Jenny had a side of stubbornness that was causing them to bump heads every now and then, but Brent knew that when they first started dating so when she got in a bad mood he would just give her some time to blow off some steam and later on they would be just fine.

We finally got Mackenzie settled in bed and we were ready to just lay around and enjoy one another. "Shay I want to just thank you for all you have done for me throughout the years. I could have lost you a long time ago, but you stuck right by my side." Mitchell said as he kissed me on the top of my head.

"I had a hard time staying firm but I had to pray and consult with God daily because it was times I had people in my ear telling me I should leave and I admit I almost did a time or two but I had to tell myself that I can't let others think for me," I told him.

"I did the things I did because I thought you were lying to me about having that miscarriage. I didn't think you were ready for kids and you were trying to watch your figure." Mitchell revealed to me.

"I knew you blamed me but I didn't think you would ever think I was capable of doing something as horrible as that," I responded to him feeling a little hurt.

"I was hurt that's all and let the devil trick me into believing that. All I really wanted was a family." He told me.

"I have to be honest about something though Mitchell. The day I lost the last baby I had received a private call from some unknown girl letting me know you guys were seeing one another and I lost it. That's why I tore up the house and how I fell on the floor the day I was admitted to the hospital."

"Bae, I don't know who that could have been because I truly wasn't seeing anyone at that time," he told me.

"Well, I didn't know what to believe. All I know is that I was hurt but since we said we were going to leave the past in the past let's not revisit it to prevent us from opening up old wounds." I told him and he quickly agreed.

"I am happy you stayed with me because I wouldn't have the two most important people here in my life today," Mitchell said as he pulled me in close and I snuggled my head under his chin and just enjoyed my husband's embrace for the rest of the night.

# The End

# How Much Can a Soul Take

*Tammy T. Cross*